THE ELEPHANT TALKS TO GOD

D1535388

Other books by Dale Estey
The Bonner Deception
A Lost Tale

THE *ELEPHANT*
TALKS TO GOD

DALE ESTEY

illustrated by
ANGELA WEBB O'HARA

Goose Lane Editions

Published with the assistance of the Canada Council, the New Brunswick Department of Tourism, Recreation & Heritage and the University of New Brunswick, 1989.

Book design by Julie Scriver
Printed in Canada by Wilson Printing

Canadian Cataloguing in Publication Data
Estey, Dale
The elephant talks to God

ISBN 0-86492-106-3

I. Title.
PS8559.S73E43 1989   C813'.54   C89-098678-9
PR9199.3.E87E43 1989

Goose Lane Editions Ltd.
248 Brunswick Street,
Fredericton, New Brunswick
Canada E3B 1G9

THE ELEPHANT SURVEYED the remnants of shattered trees, the gouged earth, and the still turbulent waves.

"You know," he said, looking up at the storm cloud hovering overhead, "a herd of us on the rampage have got nothing on you, when the mood strikes. You trying to tear down in one night what it took seven days to create?"

"Six days," noted the cloud. "On the seventh . . ."

" . . . day you rested," finished the elephant. "You gotta be patient with us lumbering beasts; after all, you didn't give us fingers so we could count."

"But I did give you memories," said the cloud.

"I know," said the elephant. "I haven't forgotten."

"And this display," added God, "looks far worse than it is. Natural forces occur to keep my earth in a happy balance. Life is already reviving and reasserting itself."

"Could you not be a bit more gentle?"

"My winds must go somewhere," said God. "As you already mentioned, even elephants go upon the occasional rampage."

"I've never done anything like this," said the elephant.

"You've not seen yourself from the ant's point of view," answered God.

THE ELEPHANT WAS HAPPY.

He moved his ears and sprayed water behind them. He grabbed trunkfulls of mud and threw them along his body. He closed his eyes and stuck his head under the river's surface, then slowly flopped over and settled on his side, stirring up currents which raced to the other shore. He blew bubbles and opened his eyes to see them break against his toenails. He wiggled his tail and scared a fish.

"Give me a squirt, will you."

The voice alarmed the elephant, and he inhaled when he should not have. He struggled to his feet, coughing.

"You're too easily startled," the voice came nearer. "Here, I'll help." The elephant felt a light touch on his back, and the coughing stopped.

"Thanks." The elephant looked around. "Where are you?"

"I'm everywhere," said God.

"I wasn't expecting you," said the elephant.

"Nobody does," answered the voice.

"I'm sorry, I've forgotten what you wanted," the elephant continued to peer around him.

"I'm over here."

The elephant looked to his left, and saw a huge boulder.

"And what I wanted was to get sprayed with water."

The elephant lumbered over to the boulder, took a large drink of water, and soaked the grey stone thoroughly.

"Thanks," said the boulder.

"You could have called up a hurricane," said the elephant.

"It means more coming from you."

"I liked you better as a cloud."

"I'm everything," answered God. "Being repetitive is a waste."

"Can you explain that to me," the elephant sat down by the boulder. "I mean, being everything and everywhere."

"Not really. It's a lot like being able to think. Your body can be in the jungle, yet you can imagine a waterhole, or the grasslands — many things at once. That's what I am."

"Have you ever been understood?" asked the elephant.

"Yes — once. About seven hundred years ago. A woman in Shansi Province in China actually figured it all out."

"What happened?"

"Nothing. She wisely kept it to herself."

The elephant hesitated, then settled more comfortably against the boulder. He felt very content, gazing at the blue sky and enjoying the coolness of the water.

"God?"

"Yes."

"Thanks for mud."

THE ELEPHANT DECIDED it was time to have a talk with God. He had been troubled for weeks, and he wasn't feeling any more assured, even at the new watering hole. He walked away from the rest of the herd and went through the jungle for half a day, until he came to a large clearing, filled with tall grass. He ate for an hour, then raised his head and trumpeted. Nothing happened, so he trumpeted again.

"I heard you," said the voice from the sky.

"Sorry."

"That's all right, I was with another elephant." A cloud hovered more closely over his head. "What seems to be wrong?"

The elephant took his time and recited all his questions and problems fully.

"It's all in the Bible," said God.

"I can't read," answered the elephant.

"That's not up to me," said God, and the cloud started moving away.

"That's it?" asked the elephant. "It's not up to you."

"Sorry," said God.

"That's not very profound," shouted the elephant at the disappearing cloud.

"You're only an elephant," answered God.

THE ELEPHANT WAS A slow thinker. When he was finally finished with an idea, it was thoroughly digested. So it was some weeks after his talk with God that he decided he may as well try once again. After all, there would not be questions if there were no answers. The other elephants shook their heads as they watched him walk away, and then returned to their grazing.

The elephant walked for half a day as he did before, had a meal of sweet grass in the clearing, and then raised his head and trumpeted loudly.

"I had a feeling I'd see you again," said a voice from the sky.

The elephant was somewhat taken aback. "I'm sorry if I called too loudly," he said.

"That's all right." A cloud hovered over his head. "I heard you through the trees anyway."

"That last time I spoke to you didn't help much," said the elephant.

"I know," answered the voice. "You expected too much."

"What do you mean?"

"I'm God," answered God. "I'm not supposed to make things easy."

"Well, I've had an idea," said the elephant.

"Fire away," answered the cloud.

"I want to talk to a Pope."

"A Pope?" The voice was mildly surprised. "Which one, we have a lot of them up here."

"Anyone will do," replied the elephant. "I figure a Pope might be able to understand my problems more, coming from earth and all."

"You're not even a Roman Catholic," said God.

"What difference does it make? I'm only an elephant, you said so yourself."

"I just threw that in to get you thinking," said God. "No slur intended."

"You mean that?" the elephant half smiled.

"Of course," said God. "I created you, didn't I? Nothing I created is without worth."

"Thanks," said the elephant.

"That's okay," said God, and the cloud started moving away. "Look, about the Pope. Come back in a month and we'll see what happens."

"You don't mind," the elephant hesitated. "I mean, about me wanting to speak to him instead of you."

"That's what Popes are for," answered God.

THE ELEPHANT WAS not oblivious to the festive season. There were carols at the mission, and incongruous baubles hanging from the large banana tree inside the walled yard. He thought that this year he would pay his respects, and journeyed half a day until he reached the special clearing. A cloud waited for him.

"It's your s . . . son's birthday and . . . and . . . " the elephant stumbled over his words. No matter how many times he talked to God, he could not overcome his shyness. " . . . I want to congratulate him."

"Thank you." The cloud descended further. "For those who believe, it is a grand time. For those who take advantage, they get their reward on earth."

"That sounds like something out of the Bible," said the elephant.

God laughed. "I thought you couldn't read the Bible."

"I can't." The elephant felt better. "You see, there's a couple of new missionaries come to the village. They're Jehovah's Witnesses, and they take turns reading the Bible to each other. They've gone through it once, and are starting again. I like that part, but some of the other things they say I don't understand at all."

"Neither do I," said the cloud.

"You mean they're lying?"

"No, not really. They mean well enough, but they expect to know everything."

"They're not much for Christmas," said the elephant.

"They mistake what they see for the meaning."

"It helps to see," insisted the elephant.

"Sure it helps," said God. "But the real belief is without seeing."

"You sent your son for us to see."

"I'm not above helping you a bit."

"Things are still pretty hard," said the elephant.

"That's life."

"God, you can be annoying."

"I know."

The elephant stood, annoyed, for a few minutes, blowing dust over himself, until he felt some raindrops. He looked up at the cloud.

"I'm waiting."

"Waiting?" asked the elephant.

"For the kicker," said God. "The Witnesses have you fired up."

"I want to see you," said the elephant, and the words raced from his mouth. "I don't have to see you, you know that. I've believed even before you talked to me. But I want to see you, it would mean so much. I wasn't around for the Baby, but cows and sheep

and things got to see Him. I can't explain but it would . . . "

"Go home," said the cloud.

"You're not angry with me," said the elephant.

"No." The cloud started moving away. "It's an honest request." The rain stopped falling. "Thank you for coming."

"You're welcome," said the elephant.

"Sing some carols," the voice was distant. "I like them."

The elephant turned and started through the woods. He ignored the tasty leaves within easy reach, and the rich grass near the brook. He wanted to get home as quickly as possible, so he could join the singing he knew was happening later in the evening.

He trotted along the trail, snapping a branch here and there in his haste, when he noted the stillness, the hush which had overtaken the forest. He slowed down, and then stopped in his tracks. He turned his head, his small eyes squinting into the brush. There was movement coming toward him, and when the trees parted he went to his knees with a gasp. Tears rolled from his eyes, and the golden trunk touched his own and gently wiped them away.

THE ELEPHANT WAS apprehensive as he finished eating the sweet grass in the clearing. He felt the timing might be bad. But God had told him to return in a month, so there he was. He noted that he was given enough time for a good meal before a cloud slowly moved across the sky, and hovered.

"Well," said the elephant.

"Well?" asked God.

"If you don't mind me saying so . . . " started the elephant.

"Speak freely."

"Well, you've really created a lot of confusion down here. Popes are dropping like flies."

"Being Pope doesn't make one immortal."

"Is everything a lesson?" asked the elephant.

"That's what life is all about."

"Then it isn't just because of me?"

"What do you mean?" asked God.

"Well . . . " the elephant did not know where to start.

"Start at the beginning," coaxed God. "That's what I did."

"To tell the truth . . . "

"I expect nothing less."

"Yes, of course. You see, when I heard about the new Pope dying, I felt guilty, because I thought that that might have happened because of me. Since I wanted some answers, I was afraid that you made him available because he could talk so easily. He once described himself as a little bird chirping a message, and you know I hear a lot of things from the birds."

"All fears based on supposition are a form of pride. I never intended the honest and useful emotion of fear to be so misused. Your concern should be about your life, let me deal with others' death."

"Sorry."

"Accept that the man's life was fulfilled by what he did. After all, I abhor waste."

"But the good that he might have done."

"He's at rest now. Allow him the good that he did do."

"I don't want to cause offence," said the elephant. "But I think I'd rather talk to him, instead of his predecessor."

"Knowledge is everywhere," said God, as the cloud

started moving away. "In a little while you may speak to them both."

"Hey, God," called the elephant. "No more surprises, huh?"

"They aren't surprises to me."

THE ELEPHANT LOOKED UP with irritation as a cloud obscured the sun, and grumbled with annoyance, waiting impatiently for it to pass and allow the early morning warmth to return.

"Up and at 'em, big fellow," said the cloud. "This is your day."

The elephant snorted with surprise, and twisted his head quickly to gaze back at the cloud. "You take a guy unawares," mumbled the elephant as he scrambled to his feet.

"In the twinkling of an eye, I believe the expression is," said God, as the cloud started to slowly move across the sky.

"You like to quote the Bible," commented the elephant as he hurried through the jungle, trying to keep up with the cloud.

"I am rather partial to it," answered God. "It's held up well over the years."

"What do you do with all the royalties?" asked the now panting elephant, whose knowledge of the publishing world was at best rather hazy.

"Plough them back into the company," answered the cloud. "Have you ever stopped to think about the upkeep of all my various buildings?"

"It's all I can do to think of keeping up with you," muttered the elephant, who was not yet quite awake, and was feeling bothered by such a hectic pace so early after sunrise. "If you'd be kind enough to give me a breather," said the elephant, doing his best to maneuvre through the thick jungle, "it'd be much appreciated."

"I gave you breath; I'll give you a breather." The cloud came to a stop, and even began to rain on the elephant, who was feeling very hot. He looked up as the shower flowed over him, and waggled his ears to get the most from the cooling water.

"Thanks," said the elephant.

"You're welcome," answered God.

The elephant stood in the rain, cooling off, waking up, looking around him at a strange part of the jungle which he rarely visited, and wondering what was going to happen.

"Idle thoughts?" queried the cloud.

"They're hardly idle," answered the elephant, whose small eyes were squinting through the rain at the cloud. "What did you mean, that this is *my* day?" The elephant gave his ears one fierce flap, and the water flew around him like a halo.

"It's something you asked a while back." The rain stopped falling, and sunshine once again struck the elephant, covering him in glistening jewels. "Two Popes of happy memory are now ready to receive you and answer your various petitions."

The elephant smiled. "You work in mysterious ways," he said.

"Touché." A chuckle came from the cloud. "We'll be on our way then."

"I don't speak Italian."

"They don't speak Elephant," answered the cloud. "But we'll work something out. Trust me."

"I do my best," said the elephant as he dutifully maneuvered through the now towering trees and thick hanging vines. Except for the cloud he followed, the sky remained clear and blue, but the deep jungle became gloomier and gloomier, and even the sounds of the birds became muffled and strange. He walked carefully, intent upon not bashing into any large trees, and was surprised to find that the cloud had stopped. He peered carefully through the darkness which surrounded him, and finally saw his destination.

"A cave?" he asked incredulously.

"For technical reasons," answered God. "Go on in, the time is not unlimited."

"How will I address them?"

"You may dispense with the numbers. Paul and John-Paul will be good enough."

The elephant inched his way into the cave, until he could see nothing at all. He stood stock-still, surrounded by the blackness.

"Hello?" he called.

"Yes, my son," a weak voice, not without humour, entered his head. "How can we help you?"

"I had the idea . . . " the elephant's voice trailed off, his mind scrambling for words. "I was going to . . ."

"Please speak up," an older voice filled the cave. "I must hear you clearly, my son, if I am to understand."

"I think there's been a mistake," said the elephant.

"That is the way of the world," commented the older voice.

"No, I mean me," said the elephant. "I feel bad about making so much trouble, and causing inconvenience and bringing you here and everything, but . . ."

"But what?" asked the quiet voice, soothing in its softness.

"You see," the elephant paused just a moment. "I thought you could give me all the answers. There's so many questions — so many — and I want to know. The grass is sweet and the water is fine, but it is not enough — there's so much to know. I'm learning — God knows — all the time, but every answer seems just to be a key in the door of yet another question. And I thought you two could . . . but . . . "

"But what?" asked Paul, interest and concern mixed in his question.

"I've found out," the elephant looked around the cave, in spite of the fact that he could see nothing. "I don't understand why, but I've found out that I'd rather discover the answers myself."

"Yet another door," said Paul. "You will pass through sundry places."

"Does it never end?" asked the elephant.

"Not even with death, my son."

THE ELEPHANT WAS standing in the special clearing, watching the fluffy white cloud come lower and lower out of the sky. He felt mildly more agitated than usual, and was wondering how he would approach God this time, for this query seemed far more foolish than any of his previous ones. Yet, God seemed to have an inexhaustible patience, and the elephant reasoned that any Deity who could put up with the incessant chatterings of the monkeys day in and day out could put up with anything. The cloud's shadow was now shading the elephant's face, and he cleared his throat.

"Ah, hello," said the elephant.

"You know," said God, "any sound of life gives me pleasure — that's why the monkeys don't bother me."

"Really?" The elephant was taken aback. "All that noise?"

"It isn't noise," said the cloud. "It's glorious life. I hear you breathing," added God, "and it soothes me."

"Really?" repeated the elephant, far less apprehensive than before. "I can do that for you?"

"Yes," said God. "You please me even with your questions; so what is it this time?"

The elephant looked stupidly at his dirty feet, and then looked back to the cloud. "I've been feeling awfully content about things lately, and . . . " he paused. "And it worries me."

"You're worried about feeling too good?"

"Yes," answered the elephant. "I'm sorry."

"I could give you a toothache," said God.

"I'm serious," insisted the elephant.

"Worry is an extreme I never meant to be," said God. "Caution yes — I think you should be careful. And preparation, yes — you should have some interest in what's going to happen, and be ready to make the most of whatever befalls you. But I never thought these would be taken to an extreme and create worry."

"I'm sorry," said the elephant.

"Another extreme," responded the cloud. "You're lucky I'm not much for brimstone, or you might get a fiery swat on your big behind." The cloud chuckled a moment. "Although I suppose it would hardly sting."

"You did give me a tough hide," reminded the elephant.

"Another expression is 'thick skin,' " said God.

"Am I to take a hint from that?" asked the elephant.

"Take the hint," said the cloud as it rose back into the sky. "And take your muddy feet, the warm sun, your full belly, the beautiful day, the joy of life, and my good blessings; and savour them and everything else down there totally until it's time for you to croak." The cloud was high and moving rapidly. "Now get going," said God.

The elephant took the hint.

THE ELEPHANT GRUNTED, yet the world slept on. The stars kept their steady gaze upon the slumbering herd, and the darkened jungle murmured with its night sounds. The elephant gave a dissatisfied twitch of his trunk, and finally rose to his feet. Taking care not to nudge any of his slumbering neighbours, he walked to the river and took a deep drink of water. When he raised his head and shook some final drops from his trunk, he noticed a fluorescent nimbus floating over to the rushing current.

"How did you know?" asked the elephant.

"I was taking a quiet turn with an angel," the cloud pulsated, "as Katherine Mansfield would say."

"I can't sleep," said the elephant.

"It will come with time; it always does."

"You made so many questions," complained the elephant.

"And as many answers," said God.

THE ELEPHANT DUTIFULLY followed the shimmering cloud as it unhurriedly moved downriver. He did not enjoy night travel, even with such a beacon before him, and he took care where he placed his feet. "I think I made an overhasty decision," he said.

"Yes?" asked God.

"I think I made a mistake in bypassing the help of the Popes; there are problems enough."

"Yes," said God.

"Aha," snorted the elephant. "You admit you made problems."

"I admit," answered the cloud, "that you perceive problems."

"Such distinction," muttered the elephant.

"I'm your God," answered God. "I'm allowed distinctions."

"Divine right?" asked the elephant.

"Even the Popes are infallible," said the cloud. "At least, that's an earthly claim. You may question them further in a little while."

"No more caves," said the elephant. "I felt as blind as a bat."

"Don't worry," answered the cloud. "I've arranged something more to my liking."

"And no mountains," grumbled the elephant. "I know your penchant for them, but I'm not scrambling up the side of a mountain in this darkness. You may be God, but you're no Hannibal."

"My, my, we're irritable when we haven't had our sleep."

"Sorry," mumbled the elephant.

"Sorry for what, my son?" asked a thin, concerned voice.

The elephant looked around in surprise, but saw only an odd twilight, hours earlier than it should be.

"It's a fault he has," answered the cloud. "He doesn't stop to think of his words and deeds, and consequently regrets his haste."

"Ah, haste," sighed an older voice. "To finally find out that there is no need to hurry."

"I want to know," said the elephant, his eyes following the dancing light, "I want to know why there is fear."

"You are still mortal, my son. That is why you fear."

THE ELEPHANT RAMMED into a tree. He looked up with some surprise, and then stepped back, shattering a wooden fence. He turned around to see what the noise was, and gouged another tree with one of his tusks. The birds were by this time in an uproar, the monkeys were scaling the nearest vines amid much chattering, and a passing hyena was laughing uproariously. The elephant ambled unconcernedly away from the havoc he had created, and started along the narrow path. He broke off branches, stomped bushes into oblivion, and uprooted a tree for the sheer joy of it. He gently snatched a startled toucan bird out of a branch with his trunk, and started to tickle him with little snorts of air. The bird began to giggle, and the elephant let him fly away. The whole jungle was now frantic, and it was not long before a cloud came scudding across the sky.

"What the hell?" asked the cloud.

The elephant looked up and smiled.

"You're drunk," said the cloud.

The elephant filled his cheeks as full as they would go, and trumpeted very loudly.

"Oh dear," said the cloud.

The elephant marched around in a tiny circle, and then trumpeted again.

"You're in love," said God.

"You got it," said the elephant, nodding vigorously.

"It had to happen sometime," the cloud sighed.

"Birds do it, bees do it . . . " the elephant starting singing.

"Even elephants with knees do it," chimed in God. "I know, I know."

The elephant grinned foolishly and stopped moving about. "Any lessons to be learned?" he asked.

"Oh yes," God sighed again. "So much."

"Well, I'm ready." The elephant kicked up his heels, a difficult task at the best of times. "Teach me."

"Oh no." The cloud started to rise into the air. "You're on your own this time. Love is for lovers to teach." The cloud moved away, casting a shadow across the elephant, who was now trying to dance on his hind legs. God had to chuckle, knowing only too well the feelings; warmed by the joy.

THE ELEPHANT SIGHED, looked around and felt that not enough notice was being taken, so pointedly, loudly, sighed again, ruffling the water in which he sat.

"If you knew the sighs I've heard," said the boulder, patiently waiting in the river.

"An elephant's sighs are as good as any."

"Yes, of course," said God, as the boulder was nudged by the elephant's shoulder. "Uniquely laced with peanut, but heartfelt nevertheless."

"You don't like peanuts?" asked the elephant accusingly.

"I like everything I made, else they wouldn't exist." The boulder settled more profoundly. "I can't, however, be held responsible for your reactions to things. I made other elephants, and you fall in love."

"Not anymore." The elephant slapped his trunk on the water.

"Don't interrupt your God," said God. "You fall in love, and that's your own doing. My job is making

elephant number one, and elephant number two. From then on it's up to your own designs and devices."

"She's a bitch," said the elephant.

"Wrong species," pointed out God.

"You know what I mean."

"I don't like inaccurate talk," said God. "I never have. I look upon speech as one of my greatest gifts."

"I'm sorry," said the elephant, who really was sorry, but especially for himself. "Things were going so well, we were even hosing each other's backs in the evening. And then she took it into her head to go and forage by herself, to leave me as she explored other mudholes." The elephant's voice became very indignant. "And I even saw her flapping her ears at other elephants. She has no right to do something like that."

"No right?" The boulder rumbled. "Birth gave her rights, and you rights, and everything else on this earth rights."

"I'm sorry," said the elephant.

"Possessiveness," snapped God. "I meant possessiveness to be guided by affection, not power."

"It works both ways," said the elephant. "I'll just ignore her, that's what I'll do."

"Even if she happens to come this way?" asked God.

"Why?"

"I feel waves against me," said the boulder. "She's entered the river above."

"I don't care," said the elephant, but he turned his head. "Upstream, did you say?"

"Yes."

"Well," the elephant lumbered to his feet. "I suppose I . . . ," he looked at the boulder and smiled. " . . . I have as much right to be there as she does."

"Definitely," agreed God. "The river belongs to everyone."

As the elephant splashed his way up river, a toucan bird settled comfortably upon the boulder.

"You want to know something?" asked God.

The toucan cocked an attentive ear.

"If we stay here, we're going to get swamped."

THE ELEPHANT HURRIED to the special clearing, an expression of great intent upon his face. Although the other elephants had long ago stopped commenting about his particular fixations, even they had passed puzzled glances back and forth. It was not a time to question him, or even to get in his way, so they continued with their grazing, yet watched carefully with their small eyes as he trotted away from the herd.

The elephant was overwhelmed by his own thoughts, and in truth, he did not even notice the perplexed animals which watched him disappear along the now well-worn path. He barely paid heed to the twists and turns through the jungle undergrowth, and at times jostled a tree which leaned too close, or trampled some errant bush unfortunate enough to crowd next to the trail. At one point, a vine tangled around his tusk, and instead of slipping away as he usually did, he irritably gave a harsh tug with his trunk and hauled the vine, and the branch it was hanging from, to the ground. He threw them aside with a toss of his head, and without breaking his stride, continued on his way.

As the elephant entered the clearing, he noticed that the cloud was already adrift in the sky, larger than usual and settling ever so slowly as he looked up.

"You've been very harsh to my domain," said the cloud. "Especially for a God who sees every sparrow fall."

"Is that true?" asked the elephant.

"I acknowledge all life returning to its source," said God.

"And then?"

"And then?" The cloud lowered even more. "And then there is no then. The silent wing is fulfilled."

"And when elephants die?" asked the elephant.

"When elephants die . . . " There was a long pause on the air. "When elephants die, my vines, my bushes and my trees all sigh with relief, and oxygen fills the air."

"You're trying to teach me something," said the elephant.

"I'm always trying to tell you something," said God. "That is why I gave you life."

"And is it successful?" asked the elephant.

"If you have moved even one pace closer to me," said God, "then there has been success in your life."

"And if I step back?" asked the elephant, taking a step backward to prove his point. "If I turn around and run, tear away as fast as I can from all these trials you seem disposed to put me through? If I enter the fields of oblivion with no more than thoughts for the sweet grass?" The elephant tugged at a mouthful of long blades growing near his hind foot, and stuffed them into his mouth. "If I did that," asked the elephant, talking around the wad of grass, "would my life be a success?"

"You would have a full belly," commented the cloud. "With a dull mind and an empty heart." The cloud lowered, its length now covered half the clearing. "Do *you* think your life would be a success?"

The elephant chewed furiously, and the cloud seemed to get a tinge darker, while a silence settled over the nearby jungle. The cloud once again shifted slightly, and the quiet voice of John-Paul filtered to the clearing, sounding unusually loud in the stillness.

"What is wrong, my son?"

"Reinforcements, eh?" gulped the elephant. "No more beast to cloud, one on one."

"You seem to be troubled, my son," said the older voice of Paul, a hint of caution in his tone.

"Of course I'm troubled," said the elephant, swallowing the grass. "I'm alive, aren't I? The two go hand in hand, like an alligator and his tears."

"A crocodile and his tears," corrected the cloud.

"You know what I mean," snorted the elephant. "Alligator, Sp. *el lagarto* — the lizard; broad heads with no tapering snouts and a special pocket in upper jaw for reception of the enlarged lower fourth tooth. Crocodile, from Gk. *krokr* — pebble + *drilos* — worm; a large, voracious thick-skinned, long-bodied aquatic reptile with a tapered snout."

"Are the Jehovah's Witnesses now reading encyclopedias to each other?" asked the cloud. "Instead of the Bible?"

"No," answered the elephant. "I've been resting outside the Mission school lately, and the decent treeshade coincides with the Sisters' nature studies. I've even found out that there are other elephants in India, although they are smaller than we are."

"Ah, the Sisters." Paul's voice had a touch of nostalgia to it. "The nuns at the Vatican took such good care of me." There was a gentle sigh. "And the meals they used to prepare even I could appreciate."

"I hear there is lots of Polish sausage now," said John-Paul.

"I didn't come to talk about food," said the elephant, looking directly at the cloud. "Or about nuns, the teaching profession or reptiles." The elephant raised his massive head as high as he could. "I've got a question — something which has been bothering me a very long time, though it sounds so simple that it almost seems silly." The elephant's huge ears were shaking in excitement, as was his small tail. "But silly or not, I want an answer; and that means no vague philosophy and no thoughtful puzzles."

"We've got a live one today," commented the cloud.

"And no jokes," said the elephant. "I've had it up to here with comments about my size and references to my trunk. A day doesn't go by when I don't hear titters coming from any number of animals as I walk through the forest. As if any of them had anything to laugh about; boy, this jungle is full of some weird looking specimens, let me tell you."

"Temper, temper," cautioned God. "I gave you all various means to survive and prosper; some can see at night and some have trunks. If you look funny to each other, it all balances out."

"I gotta question," insisted the elephant.

"All right," said God, and the cloud came within reach of the elephant. "It sounds like a winner, so let's have it. I trust it's not all sound and fury, signifying nothing."

"Is that from the Bible?" asked the uncertain elephant.

"No, it's not," said God. "Second best though, that's from Shakespeare. Talk about your magnificent creations . . . "

"My question," reminded the elephant.

"Batten down the hatches," said the cloud. "Here it comes."

"I want to know why there is the concept of 'if.' "

"God," whistled God. "That's a good one." A pronounced silence settled over the clearing, which accented the nervous twitching of the elephant's tail. It was a silence he could actually feel, yet he kept staring steadily at the cloud which hovered so close.

"Well?" asked the elephant.

"If there were no if . . ." began the cloud.

"None of that," said the elephant. "No suppositions, no hypotheses, no convoluted speculation. You have created 'if,' and we all live with 'if,' and I want to know why. Life gives us troubles enough just being what it is, but we're tortured even more by the word 'if.' We perform an act, and it turns out wrong, and that's bad enough. But then we think 'if' only we had done the other thing — when there is now no chance of ever doing it — and speculate 'if' this had happened, then this, and this, and the torment never ends. Let life be as it is."

"My son," Paul spoke, sounding kind but firm. "Life itself has 'if' in it. How can you assume to learn without any choices to choose between?"

"You are to learn from the 'if,' my son," added John-Paul. "After you have done something, and the word does not haunt you, then you have chosen wisely. When mistakes follow your deeds, 'if' should point you to another way, so you are not led to the same, or similar mistakes. Else how would you learn?"

"If there were no 'if,' " repeated God.

"I'm sorry," sighed the elephant.

"If there were no 'if,'" said God, "you would be standing here today complaining that you were nothing better than an automaton . . . *if* you could reason to come here at all."

"You're not angry with me?" asked the elephant.

"If I were angry with you, then I would be an unjust God." A wisp of cloud stroked the elephant's head. "And then, I would not be worthy of your questions." A peaceful silence returned for a few moments, and then the cloud began to lift slowly into the air. "It's time to go home now."

"Yes," agreed the elephant. "I'm tired and hungry." He started to turn toward the trail. "Thank you for coming," he said.

"We are more than willing, my son."

The elephant was just about ready to start home, when another thought crossed his mind, and a twinkle came to his eyes. "Hey," he called.

The cloud paused.

"Have you heard the latest prayer from the Vatican?"

"What would that be, my son?" questioned the quiet voice.

" 'Hail Mary, full of grace: the Italians are now in second place.' "

The cloud lingered a moment more, and then John-Paul's quiet voice once again reached the earth. "Now that forces me to ask, . . ." There was a short silence. "Did you hear what the grape said when the elephant sat on it?"

"No," admitted the elephant.

"That would be because the grape didn't say anything — it just gave a little wine."

The elephant was nodding his head in approval, chuckling slightly, when he was surprised to hear another voice.

"That reminds me," said Paul, uncertainty traced around his words. "I wonder if you heard . . . " and his voice faltered.

"Heard what?" coaxed God, mildly surprised Himself.

"Did you hear what the stream said when the elephant fell into it?"

"No," said the now curious elephant. "What?"

"Well, I'll be dammed."

And the elephant, the cloud, and a passing toucan bird, were overtaken with the resulting cheerful laughter.

THE ELEPHANT HAD been waiting in the clearing for quite awhile, and passed his time in a persistent, if somewhat odd manner. He would stand stock-still, keeping even his tail motionless, then give his front legs a slight bend, turn his head from side to side, and make a racing gallop across the grass, coming to an abrupt halt for no discernible reason. He would then look around, shake his head, dig a tusk into the earth, emit a very unelephant-like snort, and start the whole procedure over again. In fact, he became so involved in these events that he did not notice a cloud move cautiously across the sky, and come to a stop over one corner of the clearing. The cloud hovered a few minutes, and it was only as he was giving his head one of those series of shakes that he noticed it in the otherwise blue sky. He gave a foolish grin and walked over to where the cloud was descending.

"How long were you waiting?" asked the elephant.

"I am a patient God," said God. "I was prepared to stay until show-time finished."

"I suppose I looked silly."

"I'm always willing to give the benefit of the doubt," answered God. "So let's say that you looked peculiar."

"I have my reasons," said the elephant.

"I've come to expect nothing less," said the cloud. "Though I assume — hopefully — that there is more to this than meets the eye."

"I want to be a bull."

"*Oy veh*," answered God.

"I'm wondering if you can help me?" asked the elephant.

"A bull?"

"A bull."

"There have been many requests to be a bull-fighter," said God. "But you are the first who wants to be a bull."

"I've been learning to snort."

"There's more to it than that," began the cloud.

"SNORT," said the elephant.

"Not bad," said God.

"And I've been running, and learning to charge," he gave a pause for breath. "And I even have a name for myself."

"Can I guess?" asked God.

"*El Elefanté*," said the elephant.

"I was right," said God.

"How did you know?"

"It just seems to fit, somehow," answered God.

"I think I'm getting pretty good," said the elephant, none too modestly.

"Tell me something," said God.

"What?"

"Do you, er, know what happens in a bullfight?"

"Pretty well," said the elephant. "I've been watching some travelogues at the Mission, and one was about Spain."

"But do you know," asked God. "What happens at the end of the bullfight?"

"Well," the elephant looked slightly perplexed. "No, not really. The projector broke down before it was over." The elephant brightened up. "But there was talk about something to do with ears, and you know I have the largest set of ears you'll find."

"That's true," smiled God. "But." The cloud lowered even more. "Come over closer," said God. "I think it's time we had a little chat."

THE ELEPHANT WAS trying to fly.
The butterfly was trying to help.

Which made an interesting spectacle, if one is prone to the appreciation of the absurd. Or, come to think of it, makes an intriguing scene regardless, for a cloud soon came drifting from the southwest and unobtrusively stopped at a corner of the clearing.

The butterfly had tried to explain basic acrodynamics to the elephant, particularly concentrating upon the fact that the elephant's ears were deployed in the wrong section of his body, no matter how wildly he flapped them. And indeed, the elephant was making valiant efforts to raise from the earth through the use of his massive ears. He raced along, tilting his head and moving his ears at a frantic pace, the butterfly flitting a few safe feet from his trunk. Due to some garbled information he had received because of the noise his ears were making, the elephant was under the impression that his tail played an important part in the whole procedure. He waggled it back and forth erratically, thinking that if he aligned his tail to the correct angle of the updraft he hoped to create with his ears, he would soon be soaring with the effortless grace of the butterfly. But just as the elephant was starting to worry about his trunk getting caught in the tree tops as he flew past, he realized that the end of the clearing was alarmingly close.

While he dug his feet down to his toenails into the earth, he watched in amazement as the trees loomed ahead of him. The butterfly had wisely veered to the left and was lifting quickly into the air as the elephant's all too solidly earthbound body crashed through the brush and undergrowth, snapping a few of the more spindly trees in the process. He finally came to a jumbled and humble heap at the base of a large Mahogany. The butterfly hurriedly fluttered over to see if he was all right, and was reassured by the foolish grin on the elephant's face. The sight was quite comical, causing the butterfly to titter slightly as it flittered over the elephant's head. The elephant's massive ears picked up the laughter, and as he squinted to find his friend, he noticed the cloud for the first time.

"Oh God," sighed the elephant under his breath.

The butterfly was hovering over the elephant's trunk, wondering how to help, and looked up to the sky also, then glanced quizzically at a large eye while flapping air into the elephant's face.

"Thanks," said the elephant, getting slowly to his feet. "I'll be back shortly," he said, winking his eye and causing ripples along the butterfly's wing. He walked across the clearing as the cloud came closer.

"Hi," said the elephant.

"You never fail to amaze me," said God.

"Free will," reminded the elephant.

"Flying elephants were not exactly what I had in mind."

"It would make it easier on my feet," said the elephant.

"You'd play havoc with my birds," commented God.

"There's an awful lot of sky up there."

"You're an awful lot of elephant."

"Yeh," agreed the elephant. "I'm finding that out." He reached around with his trunk to rub a bump on the side of his head. "These aren't the wages of sin, are they?" he asked, touching the tender spot.

"Oh, this is hardly sin," reassured the cloud. "Folly is a much fairer description. And although the Bible has much less to say about folly than sin, it makes some interesting comments. One which may give you pause for thought is in Proverbs 15:21 'Folly is joy to him that is destitute of wisdom: but a man of understanding *walketh* uprightly.' "

"I don't mean to cause offence," said the elephant cautiously. "And I know that you are the expert, but I feel it's only fair for you to listen to II Corinthians

11:1 'Would to God ye could bear with me a little in my folly: and indeed bear with me.' "

"Touché," chuckled the cloud. "You certainly make use of that memory I gave you. Now if you would only be content with God's gifts as they are, your health would be the better for it."

"But I look at the butterflies and —"

"You don't look closely enough," the cloud shifted slightly, there was a pause. "The butterfly is light and properly proportioned, its wings created to take benefit of the air. Its weight allows it to soar with the currents, its movements take it through its life."

"In the sky it's so beautiful."

"You have your beauty."

"Not like the butterfly."

"No, you don't have beauty like a butterfly, but you have as much beauty as the butterfly."

"It's not the same."

"Had I wanted you all the same, I would have created everything the same and settled for boredom."

"I want to see what it's like up there."

"You haven't been listening," said God.

"Yes, I have, you know," the elephant smiled. "You haven't said that I'm not to try."

"No, I haven't." There was laughter sparkling around the words. "Free will, remember."

"So you don't mind?"

"No," said the cloud, starting to rise. "You won't be the first not to listen."

"And I might succeed," said the elephant.

"Yes, you might," agreed the cloud. "Such things can happen. They're called miracles."

"I think I know more of a real miracle," laughed the elephant, pointing toward the butterfly with his trunk. "She wants me to show her how to uproot a tree."

"You make a grand pair," called God, now distant in the sky. But the cloud did not move immediately away, for miracles really are rare, and they are interesting to watch.

THE ELEPHANT WAS singing to himself, watching the butterflies. They swarmed around his head and fluttered beneath his trunk, sometimes brushing against his tusks. His small eyes darted excitedly about, lost in the colours. Even so, he did not fail to notice the cloud moving slowly across the sky.

"It's like eyelashes," said the elephant.

"I beg your pardon?" asked the cloud.

"They feel like eyelashes when they touch me," explained the elephant, who raised his head to look at the cloud. The movement caused the butterflies to float away on the air currents.

"I see," said the cloud.

"Sometimes they touch my eyes," said the elephant. "With their wings."

"Yes?"

"It tickles," said the elephant.

"And do you laugh?"

"I giggle sometimes," answered the elephant. "They give me a funny look."

"Have you ever stopped to think what you sound like to a butterfly?"

"No," answered the elephant.

"Probably like the voice of God."

The elephant chuckled at that for a moment, and then grew silent. He blew a little gust of air to help a few tardy butterflies along, and looked up at the cloud.

"Can I ask you a question?"

"Everyone else does," answered God. "What have you got for me this time?"

"It's about the butterflies."

"Yes?"

"How come they only live for just a season?" The elephant looked down at the ground, then back to the cloud. "They're so beautiful, and so light . . . and friendly. And they do a great job of taking pollen everywhere and helping the flowers and plants — why, they're even making sure there's going to be food for me, isn't that right?"

"That's right," answered the cloud. "From the butterfly to you with a few extra stages thrown in."

"So why do they die so soon?"

"Butterflies don't live a season," said God. "They live a life."

"But they're gone when . . . "

"They're gone when it's their time," answered the cloud. "To a butterfly the season is their life, they expect nothing more and fulfill their existence. To the trees, your life is brief."

"You mean a butterfly thinks of its season like I think of my years?"

"Seconds or hours, long shadows or short, it's all the same kind of time," said God. "The butterfly feels he has as long a life as you."

"Really?" asked the elephant.

"Yes," said God.

"I'm glad," said the elephant.

And then God spoke to the elephant, and called him by his name, and filled his heart full of his beloved butterflies, and they soared through his blood, wingtip to wingtip, until he understood the power of their life.

THE UNIVERSITY OF WINNIPEG
LIBRARY

THE ASHDOWN COLLECTION
OF CANADIANA

THIS SPECIAL COLLECTION
OF
CANADIAN HISTORY AND LITERATURE
COMMEMORATES THE NAME
OF

HARRY C. ASHDOWN, 1886—1971

A DISTINGUISHED MEMBER OF
THE BOARD OF REGENTS FROM 1929 TO 1967
WHOSE GENEROUS BEQUEST
TO THE UNIVERSITY LIBRARY
PROVIDED THE INCENTIVE FOR
THE ESTABLISHMENT OF THE COLLECTION